DUEL MASTERS™

winning streak

adapted by mark s. bernthal

SCHOLASTIC INC.

NEW YORK   toronto   LONDON   AUCKLAND   SYDNEY

MEXICO CITY   NEW DELHI   HONG KONG   BUENOS AIRES

W9-BNK-398

If you purchased this book without a cover, you should be aware that this book is stolen property. It was reported as "unsold and destroyed" to the publisher, and neither the author nor the publisher has received any payment for this "stripped book."

No part of this publication may be reproduced in whole or in part, or stored in a retrieval system, or transmitted in any form or by any means, electronic, mechanical, photocopying, recording, or otherwise, without written permission of the publisher. For information regarding permission, write to Scholastic Inc., Attention: Permissions Department, 557 Broadway, New York, NY 10012.

ISBN 0-439-69111-7

Duel Masters, the Duel Masters logo, and characters' distinctive likenesses are trademarks of Wizards/Shogakukan/Mitsui-Kids. ©2005 Wizards/Shogakukan/Mitsui-Kids/ShoPro. Wizards of the Coast and its logo are trademarks of Wizards of the Coast, Inc.

HASBRO and its logo are trademarks of Hasbro and are used with permission. All Rights Reserved.

Published by Scholastic Inc.
SCHOLASTIC and associated logos are trademarks and/or registered trademarks of Scholastic Inc.

12 11 10 9 8 7 6 5 4 3 2 1   5 6 7 8 9/0

Printed in the U.S.A.
First printing, January 2005

INTRODUCTION

The world as we know it isn't the world around us. There are awesome creatures living in five mysterious civilizations, realms of Nature, Fire, Water, Light, and Darkness. They can be brought into our world through an incredible card game — Duel Masters!

Though many kids and adults play this game, only the best can call forth these creatures. They are known as *Kaijudo Masters*.

This is the story of one junior duelist, or *Senpai*, unique among all others. His name is Shobu Kirifuda.

1

The announcer shouted into his microphone over the cheering crowd, "There's no doubt about it, ladies and gentlemen! Shobu Kirifuda is the single greatest Kaijudo Master in the history of the world! He owns the zone!"

"Shobu! Shobu! Shobu!" chanted the thousands of fans at the Duel Masters tournament.

Strangely, one "Shobu!" sounded louder than all the others. It was Shobu's history teacher, Mrs. Koguma.

Shobu sat up wide-eyed — and now awake in the

middle of his history class. His classmates giggled at the drool oozing down his chin.

With a sigh, Shobu let go of the amazing duelist dream he'd been having, and once again faced the fact that he had been busted for sleeping in class.

That afternoon, at Rekuta's father's card shop, Sayuki wasn't surprised that Shobu's nap had earned him another week of detention. "All you ever think about is Kaijudo, Shobu," she scolded her friend. "I like dueling as much as the next person, but you don't pay attention to anything else."

Busy flipping through his dueling deck, Shobu muttered, "What? I wasn't paying attention."

Sayuki shook her head. "I rest my case. I'm worried about you, Shobu."

"Yes," Rekuta added. "Kokujo totally stomped you in your last match, and you don't even seem to care."

Mimi nodded her head in agreement.

"I *don't* care if I lose a match," Shobu shot back. "My dream is to compete as often as I can and learn everything about dueling. Then someday I'll be a Kaijudo Master, just like my father."

Rekuta's father, Maruo, wandered by and joined the conversation. "Shobu, if you're really serious about becoming a Kaijudo Master, you must compete against more difficult opponents — better players than you'll find here in my small shop."

Rekuta rolled his eyes, slightly offended. "Thanks a lot, Dad!"

Maruo laughed. "How about the Invitational Circuit?" he asked Shobu.

"There's a big official tournament this weekend," said Sayuki.

"Duelists from all over the world will be competing," added Rekuta. "Everybody who's anybody — and even a nobody like me — is going be there."

"That's awesome!" shouted Shobu. "I'll prove myself in battle against the hardcore Senpai and Kohai!"

"Uh . . . no, you won't," muttered Rekuta. "At least not this time."

"Why not?" demanded Shobu.

"You need an invitation," explained Maruo. "If you didn't apply for one, you can't compete."

"I told you about it a week ago," said Rekuta.

Shobu scoured his memory. "I don't remember that."

"Whoops! Someone wasn't paying attention again," scolded Sayuki.

"And I'm paying for it now," replied Shobu, with a disappointed sigh. "Big time!"

"I wouldn't say twenty-five dollars is *big time*," said a calm voice behind Shobu, "but you might have to mow a few lawns to pay me back."

Shobu whirled around. His mysterious mentor, Knight, stood behind him. As always, Knight wore his trademark sunglasses and a hip suit. His outstretched hand held an entry pass to the tournament for Shobu. "I assumed you'd be too busy building your deck and taking challenges to remember the Invitational competition," said Knight.

"He's a real space cadet," chirped Mimi. Her eyelids fluttered as she gazed at the handsome Knight.

"Takes one to know one," muttered Sayuki, glancing at Mimi.

"This is awesome!" shouted Shobu as he looked over the invitation. "Thanks, Knight! Don't worry, I won't let you down!"

Shobu dashed toward the door. "Come on, guys. Let's go build stronger decks for the competition!"

Shobu's friends exited the shop with him.

The strongest duelists in the world will be at this tournament, my young apprentice, thought Knight as he watched through the front window at the kids hurrying away down the street. *It will be the greatest challenge you've faced yet. But I have faith in your abilities, even if you do not yet realize your own power.*

2

Sayuki, Mimi, Rekuta, and Maruo paced nervously outside the tournament site.

"Where is Shobu?" muttered Rekuta.

"He's late, that's where he is!" complained Sayuki.

As she glanced over her friends' shoulders, Mimi's eyes popped open wide. "Wow, Mrs. Kirifuda!" she exclaimed. "You look amazing!"

The friends turned to see Shobu and his mother approaching. Mrs. Kirifuda wore a tiny cheerleading outfit in a cute shade of green. Shobu wore an embarrassed expression in a bright shade of red!

"I'm so proud of my little Shobu that I wanted him to have his very own cheering section!" said Mrs. Kirifuda. "Thought I'd do it right and break out my old cheerleading uniform from school. It still fits!"

As they headed into the building, Mimi continued to compliment Shobu's mother. "I hope I look that good when I get really old like you, Mrs. Kirifuda!"

Shobu's mom wasn't quite sure how to respond. "Thanks a lot, Mimi . . . uh, I think."

3

Duelists of all ages, shapes, and sizes roamed the lobby of the competition hall. Shobu thought he was dreaming again. "I've never seen so many duelists together in my life," he exclaimed. "Somebody pinch me!"

A sleazy duelist named Jamira overheard Shobu's comment. "I'll do more than pinch you, Dueler Dud. I'll send you home a big loser!"

Shobu lashed back, "You'll call me Dueler *Dude* after my cards shuffle you out of here, Jamira!"

"Not if I squash you before the tournament begins," exclaimed a rough, unfamiliar voice. It belonged to a duelist who was as big as a gorilla, with a face to match.

Shobu's jaw dropped in shock. Maruo leaned in and whispered, "I told you you'd be meeting some different duelists!"

"Who . . . who are you?" asked Shobu.

"I'm Takeshi Saruyama!" said the giant, with his chest puffed up in Shobu's face. "I don't need a tournament to waste you. Let's go now!"

"I'm ready," Shobu shot back. "*Ikuzo!*"

"Bring it on, you little stump," replied Takeshi. "*Koi!*"

4

A small crowd gathered around the pretournament duel in the hallway, excited about the unofficial competition.

Shobu is such an amateur Senpai, Jamira thought gleefully. *He's going to reveal his deck now and we'll know how to beat him in the tournament!*

The match was barely underway when Mimi joined Mrs. Kirifuda in a cheer. "Shobu! Shobu! He's our man! If he can't do it, no one can!"

Shobu's glare silenced them. Then he focused back on the game. "I summon Immortal Baron, Vorg! *Ike!*"

Takeshi scoffed and placed a mana card down. "Don't think that because you're a beginner I'm going to take it easy on you."

"Ha! You just wasted your turn!" cried Shobu.

"Why didn't he attack?" wondered Sayuki.

Rekuta was already scanning the duelist database on his laptop. "It says here Takeshi Saruyama is ranked fourth in his Senpai league, and that the strength of his deck comes from his ability to tame even the most ferocious Nature Civilization creatures."

"Ooh, a creature tamer," exclaimed Mimi, clueless to what that meant.

"If that's true," observed Maruo, "when Takeshi gets Deathblade Beetle into the battle zone, it's practically no contest."

Maruo's prediction came true . . . quickly!

"Game over, dude!" shouted Takeshi with a chuckle. "My mana cards are all in place, and now I summon

Deathblade Beetle! Do your thing, baby! Make Papa

proud!"

Shobu was impressed. "Cool move, Takeshi!"

"Should he compliment his opponents' moves?"

asked Mimi.

Sayuki shook her head and muttered, "At least not out loud!"

Shobu calmly placed another card down and returned play to Takeshi.

The brute yawned confidently. "This just keeps getting easier!" he bragged. "Somebody wake me when I win, because now I summon King Depthcon!"

"That's one of his most versatile creatures," exclaimed Rekuta.

Shobu gritted his teeth at that move and prepared for the worst when Takeshi shouted, "Deathblade Beetle! Double attack! *Ike!*"

Shobu could only grunt, realizing two of his shields had been nuked.

Now even more confident, Takeshi made a bold prediction. "Two more turns and this so-called duel will be over."

Shobu smiled calmly. "Don't be so sure about that, big guy. While you were concentrating all your energy summoning big, powerful creatures, I summoned those that use only a little mana. Here come their attacks . . . and there go your shields!"

"I . . . I can't believe it!" stammered Takeshi.

"Shobu broke all his shields at once!" Sayuki exclaimed happily.

"He only needs a finishing blow to end the duel," said Rekuta.

But Shobu had other plans. "I don't want to beat you out here in the lobby where it doesn't count, Takeshi. I'm going to own the zone in the real tournament today!"

Takeshi skulked away, embarrassed. But he wasn't as red-faced as Shobu when his mother and Mimi started waving pom-poms and cheering, "Shobu! Shobu! He's our man! If he can't do it, no one can! *Yaaay*, Shobu!"

Watching from a dark corner nearby, the ever-cool Knight muttered, "I wish they'd learn another cheer."

Nine games into the tournament, an Australian duelist had Shobu against the ropes. "And now, Kirifuda, I must call forth a leviathan that swallows everything! I summon King Depthcon! *Ike!*"

Rekuta cringed.

Sayuki merely marveled, "Wow. That guy's good."

"Is that bad?" asked Mimi.

Sayuki rolled her eyes. "Why don't you go work on a new cheer, Mimi?"

Maruo leaned close to Sayuki. "She won't have

anything to cheer if Shobu doesn't get out of the mess he's in right now," he whispered.

"To be truthful, Shobu," admitted the Australian, "I saw your deck when you defeated that ape Takeshi in the hallway hours ago. I knew how to play you."

Shobu refused to quit. "It's not just what you've got — it's how you use it," he insisted. "I summon Scarlet Skyterror! *Ike!* And while you're at it, *todome da!*"

"Tomato what?" asked Shobu's mom.

"*Todome da,*" Maruo explained, "It means, 'clean his clock.'"

"Another translation would be that your son just won his ninth straight tournament duel!" said Sayuki, with a wide smile. "Nice going, Shobu!"

After the shell-shocked Australian wandered away, Shobu's friends mobbed him.

Rekuta typed the final duel notes into his laptop,

then checked the tournament standings. "You're undefeated and almost in the finals, Shobu! That's fantastic!"

"Thanks," answered Shobu. "And, hey . . . how many duels have you won in your division?"

Rekuta's face puckered up. "Um . . . that would be . . . none! Zilch. Nada. I lost all ten."

Maruo patted his boy on the shoulder. "Well, that's a kind of perfect score, son."

6

Moments later, Shobu's excitement over his winning streak was lessened by the tournament announcer as he reported a couple of current leaders. "From Group F, here's another champion-in-the-making heading for the finals!" the announcer said. "He's undefeated in ten duels! Give it up for Jamira, folks!"

Jamira's greasy picture flashed on the big screen above the dueling floor.

As the crowd cheered, Sayuki muttered, "He probably cheated."

"Don't worry," said Shobu. "I can take him."

"Whoa, but look out, Jamira!" the announcer continued as a new picture appeared on the screen. "Here's another dueling prodigy who's been on fire today, also winning ten duels! Going to the finals from Group H, ladies and gentlemen, it's Toru!"

The crowd applauded again.

Shobu recognized the dueler's picture. "Hey! That's the guy Kokujo clobbered before I could take him on!"

Standing nearby, Toru overheard Shobu. "You want a piece of me?" he shouted. "I'll be waiting to crush you in the finals!"

"I'll be there!" Shobu shot back.

"What makes you so sure, Kirifuda?" a familiar deep voice asked from behind Shobu. "You still have to win your tenth match."

Shobu turned around. Behind him was Takeshi, the gorilla he'd wasted in the hallway earlier. "Oh man," said Shobu. "Don't tell me I have to dump you again!"

"Well . . . uh . . . no," the embarrassed hulk mumbled. "I lost two duels."

"Why am I not surprised?" asked Sayuki.

"But since I can't play you," continued Takeshi, "you'll face the next best thing!"

A very short duelist walked up behind the bumbling behemoth — on stilts! If Takeshi looked like a gorilla, this dude was a dead-on ringer for a chimp. "I heard you've been picking on my little brother," the chimp said in a squeaky voice. "I am the great duelist Tsuyoshi Saruyama. I placed second in this tournament last year."

"So you lost your final match," taunted Shobu.

"That will not happen in this tournament," bragged Tsuyoshi. "You and I have both won nine straight duels. Now I'll step on you to get to the finals."

"I doubt it, Mr. Second Best," Shobu shot back. "Let's duel!"

With that, Shobu's cheerleaders screamed, "See

that basket! See that rim! Come on, Shobu, put it in! Sink it!"

Shobu freaked out. "Mom! Mimi!" he screeched. "That's a *basketball* cheer! Knock it off! You're embarrassing me!"

Nearby, Knight smiled. *At least it was a different cheer,* he thought.

Disappointed, Mimi glanced at Mrs. Kirifuda. "Maybe we should stick with, 'Shobu, Shobu, he's our man.'"

Knight shook his head, thinking, *Please . . . don't.*

7

Shobu's picture finally flashed on the auditorium's big screen as the announcer introduced his next match. "Ladies and gentlemen, it's the final duel in Group A's preliminary round! Who will go to the finals? Last year's returning runner-up, Tsuyoshi Saruyama? Or this year's promising newcomer, Shobu Kirifuda! Prepare to battle, gentlemen!"

The crowd cheered in anticipation of the match.

"My little brother told me how you duel," Tsuyoshi sneered at Shobu. "You like to hold back the Scarlet Skyterror as your final trump card."

"So what if I do?" asked Shobu.

"So it won't work on me," Tsuyoshi replied. "My deck contains Nature Civilization cards. They're immune to Scarlet Skyterror. Or didn't you know?"

Always ready to learn from opponents, Shobu praised the squeaky little guy. "Wow! That's a sweet strategy, Tsuyoshi! Just when I think I know this game inside and out, I learn something new. I'll use that strategy myself sometime!"

Neither duelist played a cozy match, each launching a series of attacks on the other. Tsuyoshi grunted and summoned Mighty Shouter to break Shobu's shields. Shobu sent Brawler Zyler to counterattack. Tsuyoshi sicced Bronze-arm Tribe on Brawler Zyler. Shobu retaliated with Armored Walker Urherion against Tsuyoshi's shields.

As Rekuta frantically typed these moves into his laptop, Sayuki complained, "This is like a silly water balloon fight! They're only using offensive cards, attacking full-on with every turn."

"But you have to admit, it's exciting," replied Maruo.

"Is this strategy used often in tournaments?" asked Rekuta.

"No," answered Maruo, "and Shobu's about to find out why."

"What do you mean?" asked Shobu's mom.

"It's the amount of mana they both have," explained Maruo. "Tsuyoshi has six cards in his mana zone, and Shobu only has four."

"Is that bad?" Mimi asked.

"You'll see," said Maruo.

Sure enough, Shobu suddenly realized what Tsuyoshi had set up. "Wait . . . you have . . . Bronze-arm Tribe . . . *and* Mighty Shouter? They're —"

"Just waking up, my little about-to-lose friend?" taunted Tsuyoshi. "Hello! Anybody home? Everyone

knows Bronze-arm Tribe gives me extra mana. And when Mighty Shouter is destroyed, it's turned into a mana card instead of going to the graveyard — where you'll soon be!"

"Because you can summon as many creatures as you want if you have enough mana," muttered Shobu, as the strategy sunk in.

The situation looked bad and was about to get worse!

"I summon Bronze-arm Tribe again!" shouted

Tsuyoshi. "I have enough mana now to wipe out any-thing you throw my way, and I have you to thank!"

"An Aura Blast!" exclaimed Rekuta. "It adds two thousand power to all of Tsuyoshi's creatures."

"Now here's a little something for you!" shouted Tsuyoshi with a laugh, as he crushed one of Shobu's shields.

"Oh, no! Urherion is gone!" cried Rekuta. "And Tsuyoshi's got way more creatures than Shobu! Shobu's going to lose!"

Oh dear, thought Mrs. Kirifuda. *It's tough to cheer defeat.*

But Shobu wouldn't give up. "Quitters never win, and winners never quit!" he declared.

"Which one is he again?" asked Mimi.

"I heard that!" Shobu called to Mimi. "Just watch. I'll show you." Then he summoned two Fire Civilization creatures: Immortal Baron, Vorg and Fatal Attacker Horvath.

Tsuyoshi wasn't scared. "Too little too late, Shobu," he sneered. "Watch and learn. I summon Roaring Great Horn!"

Many spectators cheered, expecting Shobu's defeat.

"The crowd is on my side and it is time for the finishing blows," said Tsuyoshi. "I attack you with these three creatures! Break his shields!"

Shobu winced as his remaining shields were shattered.

"I won! I am the greatest! I am king!" screamed Tsuyoshi.

"He won! He is the greatest! He is king!" repeated his gorilla brother.

Shobu's mother and his friends hung their heads sadly.

8

Everybody thought Shobu was about to be knocked out of the tournament. Even Knight shook his head ever so slightly. He was disappointed . . . but he had to maintain his cool, after all.

Shobu smiled calmly.

Sayuki wasn't sure how to interpret her friend's reaction. "Is that his I'm-going-to-win smile? Or his I-just-learned-a-great-lesson-while-losing smile?"

Shobu's next move answered Sayuki's question.

"Don't order that crown yet, your highness," Shobu told Tsuyoshi. "I always save my best cards for last." He quietly placed Magma Gazer down on the dueling table.

Rekuta perked up as he typed the move into his duel log. "Whoa! Magma Gazer is a spell card that gives double breaker capacity and four thousand extra power to a creature!"

"Ooh, I'm so scared," taunted Tsuyoshi, grinning broadly. "Go ahead and use your stupid double breaker. Even if you break all my shields, you won't have enough power to attack me for the win."

"Smile while you can," said Shobu, "because like I said, I always save my best cards for last."

Shobu placed his final card on the table.

Tsuyoshi's jaw dropped. He couldn't believe his eyes. A loud gasp rose up from the crowd when they saw the creature in close-up on the big screen.

It was *another* Magma Gazer!

"Magma Gazer, double breaker!" shouted Shobu. "*Todome da!*"

Tsuyoshi had lost.

"Who's the king now?" asked Shobu.

Embarrassed, Tsuyoshi gritted his teeth and muttered, "You won today, but I still have enough wins to go to the finals, too! You won't be so lucky next time."

Shobu's brilliant comeback victory was sealed by the announcer's official statement, "Undefeated and advancing to tomorrow's finals to compete for the title of Duel Masters Battle Arena Junior Grand Champion . . . Shobu Kirifuda!"

Now the crowd was entirely on Shobu's side. "Own it!" they screamed. "Own it! Own it!"

9

Dim torch-lit hallways and rooms created an eerie atmosphere in the Temple. Cold, stark stone floors and walls did little to help warm up the place. However, in a barren room containing only a small table and chair, there was a surprising splash of brilliant color.

It was teal blue.

Teal blue *hair*.

The bright blue hair streamed down over the shoulders of a handsome young man. He was well dressed, wearing a three-piece suit, a tie, and expensive shoes.

He idly flipped through the cards in his dueling deck as a shadowy figure entered quietly behind him.

"Bored, young one?" asked the Master in his deep, sinister voice.

As always, the Master's dark robe and hood hid most of his stern face. A patch of long blond hair spilled into view.

The young man sighed. "Another day, another uninspiring exhibition match."

"I beg to differ," said the Master. "Today's outing should prove most stimulating."

The blue-haired duelist only shrugged. "It's only Toban-Jan," he replied. "He's hardly stimulating."

"It's not your opponent I'm referring to," said the Master. "It will be a spectator. Shori Kirifuda's son. You will duel today before his first tournament finals."

"Really?" asked the young duelist. "Well, this may be interesting after all."

10

In a much brighter setting, Mimi wore her colorful cheerleader outfit and practiced her latest cheer. "Chili sauce and bacon fat! Come on, Shobu, swing that bat! *Go*, Shobu!"

Now also wearing the official Kirifuda cheerleader outfit, Sayuki rejected Mimi's choice of cheers. "That needs a major rewrite, Mimi. This isn't baseball!"

"What's baseball?" asked Mimi.

They were interrupted by the sound of excitement in the competition hall below. Peering over the balcony rail, Shobu saw a crowd of screaming girls running to their seats. "What's happening?" he asked.

Sayuki's eyes fluttered excitedly. "Oh! It must be about to start!"

"I'm so glad we grabbed these front-row seats!" shouted Mimi.

"We'll be on top of everything!" said Rekuta.

"On top of what?" asked Shobu, totally clueless.

"Duh! Hakuoh's exhibition match!" said Sayuki.

"Whacko who?" asked Shobu.

"Ha-ku-oh," corrected Rekuta. "How can you call yourself a duelist, and not know the name of the world champion?"

"He's so totally dreamy," said Sayuki with a sigh.

"So totally superdreamy," agreed Mimi, with a bigger sigh.

Rekuta's father praised Hakuoh's statistics more than his blue hair. "He's undefeated in official play," said Maruo, "and the strongest player in the Duel Center. He's brilliant!"

"And totally superdreamy," added Mimi.

"I heard you the first time," said Shobu, annoyed and a little jealous. "What's so great — ?"

The announcer interrupted. "Ladies and gentlemen, we have a rare treat for you this afternoon before we begin our Junior Duelist tournament finals! You'll see a special exhibition match with a duelist who can really own the zone!"

"Not *my* zone!" scoffed Shobu.

"This young man really needs no introduction," the announcer continued. "His luminous three-piece suit and teal-blue hair says it all! He's undefeated, undisputed, and under contract to several major hair-care and apparel companies. You know him, you love him! Ladies and gentlemen, Hakuoh!"

The crowd went nuts, including Shobu's mother. "My, he's quite —"

"Yeah, I know, Mom . . . ," broke in Shobu. "Dreamy."

Mimi, Sayuki, and Shobu's mother jumped to their feet. "Five foot two-oh, hair of blue-oh. Who's the best? It is Hakuoh!"

Shobu buried his head in his hands and muttered, "So much for, 'Shobu! Shobu! He's our man!'"

Hakuoh made a grand entrance between two groups of men dressed in white. They were three rows deep on each side and standing at attention.

"Wow!" said Rekuta. "There's Hakuoh's dueling team — the White Soldiers. Strongest in the world."

"Vanity, thy name is Hakuoh," said Shobu. "Is this a duel or a Vegas floor show? I can't believe I have to delay my first tournament finals for this!"

"And now . . . ," the announcer rumbled over the loudspeakers, "give it up for Hakuoh's worthy opponent! He's a duelist who really cooks, in and out of the arena. He's got a wok and he's not afraid to

use it. You may know him from his fabulous line of frozen cuisines, but today he's hoping to serve up a little crow. Please welcome the champion from China, Toban-Jan!"

Through a cloud of smoke and fire, Toban-Jan also entered the arena with pizzazz. He pointed at Hakuoh, shouting, "Hey! I came all the way from Shanghai to cook you! And nothing's easier to prepare than ham!"

Rekuta's fingers zipped across his laptop keyboard. "I checked the net for Toban-Jan's stats. Wow, he's finished nearly every duel within 10 minutes!"

"So he's a swift attacker," said Shobu.

Rekuta read the screen. "Yep. His specialties are swift attacks with a deck full of Fire Civilization cards."

"Just like Shobu," said Maruo.

"*Just* like me," mumbled Shobu. He leaned forward over the railing. The match had suddenly become much more interesting.

11

Both duelists began loading their mana zones. Finally, Toban-Jan cried, "Let's throw a couple of shrimp on the barbie! I summon Brawler Zyler and Fatal Attacker Horvath."

Hakuoh countered by summoning Dia Nork, Moonlight Guardian.

Rekuta frantically typed the moves into his database. "Hakuoh summoned a blocker. Cool!"

"He knows his way around," agreed Maruo. "Now Toban-Jan has to attack carefully."

Shobu smiled. "But don't underestimate a guy who can pull so much cutlery out of his pants!"

"Now it's time to use my secret ingredient," shouted Toban-Jan. "I summon Rothus the Traveler!"

"Great move," whispered Shobu. "Toban-Jan is a man with a plan! Each card has to send one of his creatures to the graveyard! Brawler Zyler's out, but now Dia Nork is gone too. Big turnaround!"

"The oil is just hot enough for frying and something smells delicious!" Toban-Jan shouted happily. "Here comes the specialty of the house — Fatal Attacker Horvath! *Ike!*"

"There goes one of Hakuoh's shields," said Sayuki.

"Thank goodness it didn't mess up his hair," whispered Mimi.

As the match progressed, Rekuta discovered more interesting statistics on his laptop. "That last attack

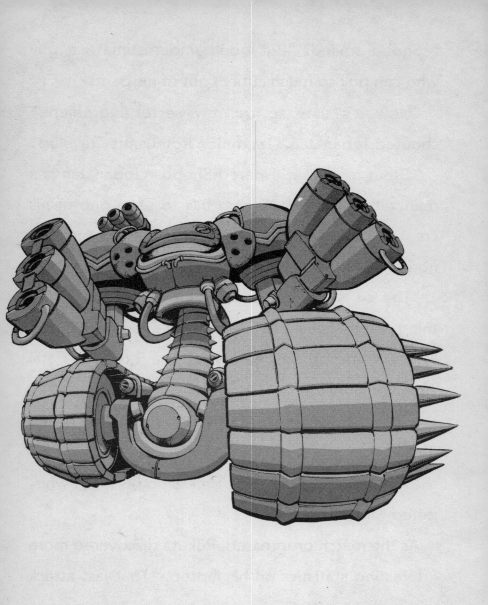

by Toban-Jan is one Shobu's used twelve times. They're more alike than I thought!"

"Doesn't surprise me," said Maruo, "Their deck structures are almost identical."

Hearing that, Shobu moved to the edge of his seat, drawn into the contest as though he was dueling Hakuoh himself!

12

Shobu winced as Hakuoh climbed back into the match by summoning two blockers — Emerald Grass and Senatine Jade Tree. "Toban-Jan could crush those blockers with Scarlet Skyterror," he said.

"Oh, I love that band!" squealed Mimi.

Sayuki rolled her eyes. "Mimi, what color is the sky in your world? Scarlet Skyterror is a *card!*" Then she turned to Shobu. "I hear you, but Toban-Jan needs a lot more mana to summon Scarlet Skyterror."

"You're right," agreed Rekuta, typing duel moves

into one window while checking statistics in another. "Both have played the same number of years and Hakuoh is undefeated. But if Toban-Jan can hang in there until he has enough mana to summon Scarlet Skyterror —"

"He can win!" Shobu exclaimed.

But just after Toban-Jan served up Armored Walker Urherion, Hakuoh rocked the auditorium with his counter move.

"Yikes!" cried Shobu. "Urth, Purifying Elemental! It's an Angel Command with six thousand power."

On Toban-Jan's turn, he could only lay a card in his mana zone.

Play went back to Hakuoh. "I now summon Szubs Kin, Twilight Guardian," he declared.

Shobu was astounded. "Am I seeing straight?" he asked. "Hakuoh just summoned another blocker using five mana!"

Maruo smiled. "Takes your breath away doesn't it? It's Hakuoh's favorite formation, called The White Terror."

"Shobu looks nervous," Mimi whispered to Rekuta.

"Hakuoh might defeat a deck and strategy very close to his own," Rekuta answered.

Sure enough, Hakuoh made his move. "Urth, Purifying Elemental. *Ike!* Double-break his shields."

"There go two of Toban-Jan's shields," said Rekuta. "His goose is cooked."

"Pretty Boy hasn't won yet," replied Shobu.

Though he couldn't have heard him, Toban-Jan certainly agreed with Shobu. "Do you find my cooking bland, Hakuoh?" he joked. "Well, let's kick it up a notch with my secret seasoning. I summon Super Explosive Volcanodon!"

"You're still no match for me," taunted Hakuoh.

No match, my apron! thought Toban-Jan. *My spice rack isn't empty yet. I've still got Scarlet Skyterror!*

Shobu pondered Toban-Jan's strategy as if it were his own. *If he has Scarlet Skyterror, he'll send all of Hakuoh's blockers to the graveyard! Then he'll break his shields easily. He just needs one more mana and he wins!*

"The next turn, I'll be feasting on victory," insisted Toban-Jan confidently. "And you'll be eating crow, Hakuoh!"

But Hakuoh had one final trick up his sleeve. He calmly played a card, declaring, "Holy Awe. Finish it."

Shobu's jaw dropped. "I've seen that play before! Knight used it on me the first time I played him! Holy Awe is a spell that taps all of an opponent's cards. Now all of Toban-Jan's creatures are vulnerable!"

Hakuoh took advantage of that vulnerability. "I attack with Urth, Purifying Elemental! *Ike!* Next, I attack with Szubs Kin, Twilight Guardian. *Ike!* Now, Emerald Grass attack! *Ike!* And Senantine Jade Tree, attack! *Ike!*"

Hakuoh smiled and turned play over to Toban-Jan, who made a final effort to win, sending all Hakuoh's blockers to the graveyard. But the price was too great. In the end, Toban-Jan didn't have enough creatures to attack Hakuoh! Finally, Toban-Jan slumped. "Stick a fork in me, baby. I'm done."

The crowd — including Shobu's cheerleaders — went wild, shouting Hakuoh's name over and over.

Shobu was crushed. "All we needed was one more turn."

"All I needed was one more turn," mumbled Toban-Jan. "Nice work, Hakuoh. You're one sharp duelist."

The blue mop-head sneered at his defeated foe. "I wish I could say the same about you."

The announcer closed the exhibition. "Junior duelists, that should psych you up for some intense finals play, and we'll announce the match-ups in just a bit. But first, let's put our hands together for two terrific duelists — Toban-Jan and the still-undefeated Hakuoh!"

Despite the wild crowd noise, Maruo's mind jumped to the junior tournament about to resume. "We'd better get you focused on your own play, Shobu," he said, turning toward the boy.

But Shobu was gone!

13

Down on the dueling floor, the crowd scrambled to catch a final glimpse of Hakuoh. Shobu scrambled harder, pushing through the throng. "Hey, Hakuoh! Wait up!" he shouted.

Shobu broke past Hakuoh's body guards, nearly reaching the duelist champ before two White Soldiers snatched him into the air. Hakuoh turned to see what the disturbance was about.

"I have to admit, Hakuoh," said Shobu, "you owned the zone today! But I'm about to win the junior tournament, and after I do, I want to duel you! I'm calling you out! *Kettou da!*"

Hakuoh calmly brushed some blue hair out of his eyes. "And you are . . . ?" he asked.

"I'm Shobu Kirifuda! You'll be hearing a lot about me soon!"

Hakuoh smiled, turned, and walked away without a word.

Shobu struggled to free himself, while shouting at Hakuoh. "Hey! Come on! This is no way to treat a future champion! Wait! You forgot to give me your phone number! I'll call you! We'll do lunch at the Temple!"

Hakuoh never looked back.

14

In a dark hallway under the stadium, Hakuoh met Knight, who was casually leaning against the wall. "So that's Shobu Kirifuda," he said.

"Mm-hmm," replied Knight quietly.

"Spirited little tyke," said Hakuoh. "Reminds me of myself, before the weight of reality smashed my joyful, childlike innocence. It will be a pity when I have to crush him."

"Yeah, he's young and rough around the edges," said Knight. "But his potential is absolutely staggering. Trust me on this one."

Hakuoh dismissed Knight's opinion with a wave of his hand. "Whatever. Why don't you stop by the Temple some time for a game? I could use some real competition."

Knight shook his head. "Be patient, Hakuoh," he muttered. "I promise you, you will get it."

Without looking back, Hakuoh resumed walking over to his waiting helicopter.

Get the inside edge!

Look for D-MAX membership offers in the Duel Masters Starter Set or check online at Duelmasters.com

DuelMasters™

TRADING CARD GAME

The Wizards of the Coast logo is a trademark of Wizards of the Coast, Inc. in the U.S.A. and other countries.
The **Duel Maste** logo and characters' distinctive likenesses are TM & © 2004 Wizards of the Coast/Shogakukan/Mitsui Kids ShoPro